Coyote
Not-so-clever

Native American stories
retold by Barbara Beveridge

illustrated by Ali Teo

Learning Media

1
Coyote Gets His Tail

That Coyote, he thinks he's so smart, so clever. But really, he's not-so-clever. He's always getting himself into trouble. Did you hear how he got that droopy tail of his?

It happened long, long ago. In those days, the only bird with feathers was an eagle who lived on top of a high mountain. The other birds wanted the eagle to share his feathers with them, but the mean old thing wouldn't let them have even one. So the birds decided that the only way to get the feathers was to kill the eagle.

"I'll help you," said Coyote. Of course, Coyote just wanted some of those feathers for himself. And, as usual, he was looking for trouble.

They all took their bows and arrows and went up the mountain. By the time they got there and killed the eagle, it was dark, so they decided to wait till morning to share out the feathers. "I'm going to have first pick of the best feathers," Coyote thought to himself, "so I'll have to stay awake all night till the sun comes up." But he was so tired that he soon fell asleep.

When the sun came up, Coyote was still asleep. He was woken by the noise of all the birds. They were chattering and showing off their new feathers. "What do you think, Coyote?" they called. "Don't we look beautiful?"

"Oh, no!" cried Coyote. "Did you leave any feathers for me?"

"Sorry, Coyote," said the birds, "but you know that feathers wouldn't look good on you. We've got something else for you instead. The eagle had this thing hanging from behind him. We thought it would be just right for you."

The thing was a long and droopy tail. It looked like an old brush, but Coyote was delighted. He stuck the tail on and dragged it about on the ground. He thought he looked just wonderful.

He still does!

2
Coyote Learns to Sing

One sunny morning, Coyote went out hunting with his new tail dragging behind him. On the way, he passed an old pine tree. Hooked onto the trunk of the tree was a locust. The locust was happy singing in the sun – until Coyote came along. "Hullo there, Locust," called Coyote. "That's a fine song you're singing. I wish you'd teach it to me."

"You'd better listen carefully, then," said the locust rather grumpily. And he sang his song to Coyote.

"Let me see if I've got it right," said Coyote. But he had forgotten half of the song, and the locust had to sing it again.

When Coyote finally got the song right, he went on his way. He was singing at the top of his voice and was not looking where he was going. All of a sudden, he tumbled head over heels into a large hole. The hole had been dug by Gopher.

Coyote was angry. "Why did you dig such a big hole, you stupid gopher?" he yelled.

"To stop you making that noise," said Gopher.

"Noise!" said Coyote. "I was singing."

"Singing! Is that what you call it?" laughed Gopher as he disappeared into his house.

"You idiot!" said Coyote. "Now I've forgotten what I was singing. I'll have to go back to Locust and ask him to sing it again."

The locust was still hooked onto the trunk of the pine tree. He wasn't too happy to see Coyote. "Please, please, sing your song again," said Coyote. "I've forgotten how it goes."

"I'll sing it for you once more, but only once," the locust said. So Coyote learned the song and went on his way.

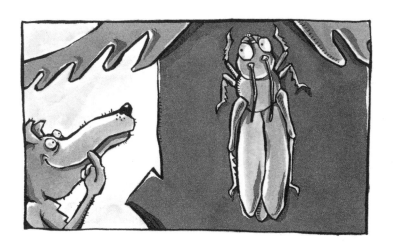

He hadn't gone far when a flock of pigeons flew up from a clump of bushes right in front of him. "What a noise you're making!" the pigeons cried. "Go away and leave us in peace. We can't hear ourselves think." And they flew away before Coyote could complain. Coyote was so angry that he forgot the locust's song again.

But the wise old locust guessed that
Coyote would be back. He was ready with a
trick. He split his skin open at the back.
Then he climbed out and left the skin
hanging on the pine tree. He stretched his
wings and flew away to another tree.

Coyote got to the old pine tree and
called, "Hullo there, Locust! Sorry, but I've
forgotten the song again. Will you sing it
for me?" There was no answer. "I've said
that I'm sorry, Locust. I want you to sing
the song again." Still no answer. "Now,
look here, Locust, if you don't talk to me,
you'll be in big trouble," Coyote yelled.

When there was still no answer, Coyote grabbed the locust skin with his teeth. He bit hard, so hard that he crushed his teeth together. Some of his teeth went into his gums, and some were pushed aside. It was Coyote who was in big trouble. "Ow! Ow!" he yelled. "My poor teeth!" He ran to the stream, where he could cool his aching mouth.

Coyote still has crooked teeth, and Locust still likes to sing in the sun. Every now and then, he splits his skin open and climbs out of it. He leaves the skin hanging on a tree and flies off to another place – where he hopes he'll be left in peace!

3
Coyote and the Mice

One day, Coyote was out walking in the forest. He was showing off his tail and trying to sing the song the locust had taught him. Suddenly he saw a band of mice. They were running toward him, calling at the top of their squeaky little voices, "Hurry! Hurry, Coyote! A terrible hailstorm is on its way. You must get your bag ready."

Now, this was a puzzle to Coyote. Why would the mice want to help *him*? You see, he wasn't very popular with the mice. They said that Coyote had killed some of their children. Coyote said that it had been an accident. He'd rolled over on them when he was asleep. He felt bad about it, but it was their own fault. That's what *he* thought.

Anyway, Coyote saw that all the mice had little buffalo skin bags with ropes. "What are you going to do with those?" he asked.

"We'll each climb into a bag, throw the rope over a branch, and pull ourselves up into the trees," one of the mice said. "We'll be safe from the hail there."

"That's a clever idea," said Coyote.

"Here," said another mouse, "we brought a big bag and a rope for you. But you'll have to hurry, Coyote. That hail will be here soon."

"Right," said Coyote, who was getting nervous. "Give me the bag. Quickly!"

Coyote tied one end of the rope to his bag. Then he tried to throw the other end of the rope up and over a big strong branch. It missed and hit him on the nose. He tried again and got it right this time. He climbed into the bag and pulled himself up on the rope until he was swinging in midair. Finally, he tied the other end of the rope onto the bag and hid himself inside.

"We're all in our bags now, Coyote," yelled the mice. "We're just in time. Here comes the hail!" And, laughing to themselves, they picked up stones and threw them at Coyote's bag.

"Ow, ow!" howled Coyote.

"Oh, oh," squeaked the mice, "the storm is getting worse, and the hailstones are bigger!" And the stones rattled against Coyote's bag.

"Ow, ow!" Coyote howled.

"Be brave, Coyote," called the mice. "You're bigger and stronger than us."

Soon the mice were tired of throwing stones. One of them called out, "Thank goodness! The storm is over. We can get out of our bags now." Coyote undid the rope and let his bag down. "Come on, Coyote, you can get out now. The storm is over, and we're still alive."

Coyote crawled stiffly out of his bag and looked around him. The sky was blue, and the ground was dry. And why were all those stones on the grass? The mice stood there, watching quietly. Coyote stared at them, feeling very stupid indeed. He could see what had happened and why. "You tricked me," he said, "but I suppose I deserved it."

Coyote went home to rest his aches and pains – before he got into trouble again.

4

Coyote and Fox

Coyote and Fox were enemies. This is how it happened.

Fox had caught a rabbit for his dinner. He built a fire, let it burn down, and then covered the rabbit with hot ashes. While the rabbit was cooking, Fox decided to have a sleep.

Soon Coyote came along and smelled the meat cooking. "Mmm! Mmm!" he said. "That smells like rabbit." He saw Fox asleep and crept over to the pile of ashes. Quickly he pulled out the meat and ran behind a bush. Coyote ate all the meat, every last little bit.

When Fox woke up, he knew that Coyote had stolen his dinner. He saw Coyote's tracks as clear as could be.

After that, Coyote knew that Fox would be mad at him, so he kept out of his way. But one day, when he was out walking, who should he find but Fox. Fox was standing at the bottom of a cliff, pushing at it with all his might. Before Coyote could run off, Fox called out, "Thank goodness you're here! I can't hold on much longer. The cliff is going to fall. If you don't help me, we'll both be crushed."

"What a story!" said Coyote. "You don't expect me to believe you."

"Look at those stones falling down," said Fox. It was true. Stones were falling from the top of the cliff, and that was enough to scare Coyote. So he stood beside Fox and leaned against the cliff and pushed and pushed.

"Push harder!" Fox cried.

Coyote pushed for all he was worth. "We can't go on like this," he said.

"Do you think you're strong enough to take all the weight while I go and find a log to prop up the cliff?" said Fox.

"All right!" said Coyote. "But hurry!"

Fox moved slowly and carefully away from the cliff. "I'll be as quick as I can," he said, "but it may take me a while to find a log that's big enough." And he rushed off, out of sight.

Coyote kept on pushing. The sun grew hotter and hotter, and his body ached and ached. "Where's that Fox got to?" he moaned.

The day went on, and then it was evening, and still Fox hadn't returned. Coyote couldn't push any longer. He jumped away from the cliff and ran. Then he stopped and looked back. Nothing had happened – no rumbling, no falling rocks.

Now Coyote knew that it had all been just a trick, and Fox had made a big fool of him. "He'll be down at the lake, having a drink," Coyote thought. "I'll catch him!"

Sure enough, Fox was at the lake, standing in the moonlight. "Just calm down and have a drink," he said to the angry coyote. "Then you can help me to get my maize cake from out of the water. A strong swimmer like you will be able to reach it."

Coyote saw what seemed to be a large, yellow maize cake lying in the water, out in the middle of the lake. "I was on my way back to you," went on Fox, "when I stopped for a drink. I slipped, and the cake fell into the water. Now it's floated too far for me to reach."

Coyote didn't stop to think. He was feeling hungry after his long day. He jumped into the water and swam and swam. He looked this way and that for the maize cake, but of course he couldn't find it. There was no maize cake, just the reflection of the full moon.

Fox had made a fool of Coyote again, and there he was, running into the trees, laughing his head off. And there was Coyote Not-so-clever, cold, wet, and miserable, telling himself to try and keep out of trouble in future.

But, of course, he'll never learn!